Novelette

SYMBIOSIS 1908

By Alex Pusineri

To my father

Pierre Joseph Marius Pusineri
and his love for Mathematics

Acknowledgments

My gratitude to:

Kenneth and Helen Loverme

Carlos Fletes

Gabriel Nee

Daniel Quevillon

Alban Mathevet

The all mighty and precious Wikipedia

Prologue:

On the early morning of Tuesday June 30th, 1908, at 7:14 a.m. local time, a very powerful explosion has been reported in a remote location in Siberia, Russia.
"...The explosion registered on seismic stations across Eurasia. ...The shock wave knocked people off their feet and broke windows hundreds of miles away. ...Over the next few weeks, night skies were aglow such that one could read in their light, sometimes called "bright nights."
This case has been recorded as the "Tunguska Event" for being located in the area of the Stony Tunguska River. As of today, many theories have been suggested for the cause of it but none brought unanimity.
All the facts described in this story are based on this real event.

Table of contents

[Russian Empire, Siberia, July 1ˢᵗ, 1908]

Alone

It woke up. Disoriented for few decimals. Alone. *It* spontaneously tried to sense if any of *Like-It* were nearby. Nothing. *It* pushed *its* sensory abilities at the maximum to expand the range of *its* perception. Still nothing. Just a loud silence. Where was *It*? What is this ground? The basic memories in *its* cells indicate that *It* should have been inside the Vessel, in the Harmonization room, where all the newly-created *become* and are awakened when necessary, ready for the synchronization—not somewhere else. Was *It* fully awake? Is this the real reality? Disturbed. *It* should have self-connect with the other *Like-It* by now. No Link, no Embrace, just emptiness. They would never have left *It* awaken unattended, without performing updates on *its* cells, unlinked from all or simply unprepared for *its* Awakening. Isolated. What caused this? Could this abnormal situation be temporary? Any more *Like-It* active and coming back? Time units are passing. Doubting. The aloneness in itself was a very serious warning. The primary projection is pointing toward a negative equation. Something went absolutely wrong. All the other *Like-It* are most likely diluted.

[Switzerland, July 11ᵗʰ, 1908]

Noctilucent clouds

It was 03:14 a.m., at the conclusion of an enlightened discussion
about Henri Poincaré's work with his dear friends from the
Academy, when he decided to walk them out and get some fresh air
for himself. After high praises of their long debate and cheerful
goodbyes, he simply stood there, by the door step, watching them
going their way, grasping this pleasant and softly warm night, like
they often have beginning of July in central Europe. A mild breeze
with appeasing scents is chartering the summer season's optimism,
encouraging him to go for a little walk. After few steps, he realizes
that something is unusual. Another few steps, and he sees it: "The
light! The light is different! Why is it so bright?" He checks his
trusted omega pocket watch but sunset is still few hours away, so
why so much brightness in the heart of the night? After a quick look
up, he notices that the clouds are uniformly luminous and dispensing
enough light to let you literally read a book without the help of an
artificial light. The spectacle is a bit awkward when you really think
about the actual time, and he didn't recall any sight of these glowing
clouds before—it is a first for him. Can it be an unusually bright
aurora borealis, above the clouds, generating that much luminosity?
Probably. Although he never heard of one that south in the
hemisphere. His scientific mind is now quite intrigued by this
unexpected little enigma. "Today, I'll make inquiries about this
intriguing phenomenon, there must be an explanation of some kind.
Atypical brightness like this one does not seem completely natural
to me." That thought, he slowly walks back home, heads up,
observing these riveting, noctilucent clouds, for a well-deserved rest.

The shock and adjustment from the brutal awakening lasted less than few time units. *It* acknowledges that *its* current location is on the ground of an unknown planet, with the very higher view all blue and a thick layer of livable air. Possibly the originally targeted planet. Mining knowledge from the basic memory banks embedded in *its* cells should bring precious advices, and push the equation of survival in the positive levels. *It* was left inside *its* own spherical and translucent nacelle, which is missing 17 percent on the upper side section, allowing a healthy mix of nitrogen and oxygen to enter. Aside from being extant, it is a crucial and positive data, a welcome breathe from this new world. Added to the equation. Likewise, unexpected tiny drops of water are heavily suspended in the air, making *It* feel at ease. Added too. Gravity is also falling in the suitable ranges, as a partner that will let *It* uses *its* different states, not as a burden at all. Added. These vital data are consistent with the targeted planet's estimated potential.

Since the small crack is conveniently located at the top of the nacelle, *its* whole unity is still safely contained inside the familiar habitat, now serving as a temporary protective shell. Perplexed. At this instant, a set of 3 evidences appeared contradictory. 1, *It* is in liquid state, *its* natural morphology under normal conditions, like every newly-created are when they are awakened. 2, *its* protective nacelle is made of a very strong matter, not easy to breach. 3, the safety mode, when *Like-It* shift to the solid-glass state to face any kind of danger, is not in effect. The force that could have done the opening in the nacelle should have triggered the safety-glass state as a defensive and protective mechanism. Deducting. The logical explanation simply comes to this: *It* must have been resting on this ground for some time. *It* must have shifted into the glass state during the incident, then back to the liquid and normal state, when danger faded away. Evaluating that duration will require additional data.

The light. The rays of light from the unique bright star high above are a precious gift, a feast, a bath of wellness, allowing the photosynthesis process to perform and sustain *its* organism efficiently. Another key and prized data. Added. Under the light, *its* cells are nourished, replenished and fully functional, granting *It* a clearer computing vision and confidence. Gathering. Maybe the heat is strong at times but nothing *its* cells can't handle so far. It's when a dark time arrives that *It* envisions a different outcome without any light available. If *It* cannot maintain a constant contact with a light source, *It* will be forced to retreat into the glass state, in a standby mode, stranded—limiting *its* options. Negative data. Added. So, when the light is back again, *It* realizes that it's most likely a regular cycle, where the light replaces the dark and so on. Added. These dark periods are a very serious handicap, as well as these sharply fluctuating temperatures between light and dark, when the coolness is interfering with the clarity of *its* vision. Concerned. The need for a steady and reliable energy source to stay at the optimum alertness level, even during the dark periods, is now becoming a great priority. *Its* memory cells are signaling an alternative solution for a secure and full time flow of energy. *Its* instinct is also inviting to follow the same direction: achieve a symbiosis. *Its* computing vision, who had already started to compile the collected data into a preliminary projection, reached the same result: staying safe, under the light, observe, initiate a symbiosis as soon as possible. The switching to the bacterial photosynthesis with an indigenous partner should provide a steady energy feed. New objective: finding the best suitable native life form, if any available in the nearby surroundings, to bypass these dark cycles' handicaps and secure a long term survival. However, all things around *It* have been mainly inanimate or extremely small to be accommodated with, making *It* wondering if there is a sizable native, able to move freely on his own, with an evolved conscience.

[The scenery is a strong statement of a recent and very powerful explosion. The scale of the devastation is a call for humility. The flattened forest now let the sky reign over her previous empire. Silence, lifelessness, broken and burnt trees everywhere are dispensing a mourning grip.]

At this point, even if *It* still hasn't linked with any other *Like-It*, *It* knows *It* doesn't need to look for other nacelles since *It* was the only one created after their departure—meaning that only one *Like-It* has diluted before the incident. So, *It* simply decides to start a second scanning and sensing of this new environment, now able to absorb more details. Silence is everywhere, no sounds of life yet. Although this world should be lively, it is either empty, dead or on pause of life forms. Obvious clues of a truly violent blast could be the reason and would also explain the breach in its nacelle. Adding a new line in the equation: the disappearance of the Vessel, plus, finding itself outside and totally alone, plus, the devastation of the surroundings, equal a 97.3 percent probabilities that *its* unique Vessel was annihilated. Disgruntled. Another negative contact attempt with this particular planet.

The scanning shows that *It* is resting near the limit of the blast radius, with a wide view of the vast damages on one side, and the spared matter as it appears to be before, on the other side. Previously long brown cylindrical and vertical matters with green tops, are now blackened and flattened in the opposite direction of the distant explosion's center point. Sparse areas on the preserved ground side, are covered and linked with a multitude of smallish colorful matters, most likely non-organic and sedentary, conceivably in synergy with the ground. Promising. Physical contact will be required to learn if these matters are self-conscious or just basic elements. Incoming new string of data. The air around *It* starts to move unevenly, at a very different speed and force. That instability will be a serious concern when the time for displacement will come. Added.

Intriguing mystery

After few hours spent in deep sleep, he wakes up well rested and ready to investigate the glowing mystery. A rapid toilette, followed by a hot cup of tea and the last boiled egg flavored with sparse grinded cinnamon, get him on the way. "First, the newspapers." The kid at the corner of the street should have the foremost one today. Once the transaction done, he glances through it quickly but find nothing. No extra bright clouds mentioned anywhere. "Bizarre." Thinking for few seconds, "The fire station! They should know something about it if it was caused by a building on fire in town or in the surrounding forest." On its way to the station, he observes the people's behavior but nothing is out of the ordinary, everything is as regular as any other day in this calm city of Bern. Seven minutes later, at the fire station, which appears very calm too, he hails a fireman entering a side door of the building.

"Sir? Excuse me sir! I was wondering if I can ask you a quick question about last night."

"Yes sir. How may I help you?"

"Well, last night at around 3:30, I was walking down my street to get some fresh air when I realized it was way too bright for that time of the night. So I've been wondering since then what could have triggered this estrange glow? Was there a big fire somewhere?"

"Oh no sir, the brightness was too evenly spread for a fire. Haven't you heard of the big explosion in Siberia about ten days ago?"

"Explosion? In Siberia? Not at all! You mean in the Russian Empire? Why does it have anything to do with us over here?"

"Well, apparently, there were some kind of object, a meteorite I think, that crashed in the middle of nowhere in Siberia, devastating all the forest and surroundings, up to 50 miles I heard!"

"What? Remarkable! Why didn't I hear about it?"

"I don't know sir, but it's kind of a mystery now. They say they are not sure if it is the clouds with suspended dust traveling toward us and northern Europe, or the light passing through high-altitude ice particles that are causing these very bright nights."

"Fascinating… You mean last night was not the first one?"

"No sir, it started two nights ago."
"By the venerable Socrates, Where was I? I managed to miss this one too!"
"Don't feel bad sir, most people don't know. I first heard of it when our chief explained it to all of us in case someone curious would ask about it!"
"That's a very good attention from his part. An explosion in Siberia... But you are sure he did not mention the possible reflection of an aurora borealis, above the clouds, that could have caused this phenomenon? Siberia is far away you know!"
"I don't think so sir, I'm repeating what our chief explained to us".
"Of course, of course. Well, I appreciate your help on this matter sir. Thank you kindly for your time."
"Pleasure to be at your service sir."

Self-motion, even for a short distance, is a delicate and dangerous proposition for *Like-It*. It's not a natural or a spontaneous ability but a rather painstaking option, a burden. Plus, it can only be achieved by shifting into the gas-vapor state because the liquid state is too heavy to control. The entire process, from shifting, then being able to hold *its* Whole together, to finally reach the objective, will demand *its* undivided attention. It is after all, a very volatile state to be in. A sudden strong force of air could disrupt and disperse *its* whole unity in different directions, which in turn, would make *It* loses *its* consciousness or maybe worse. Habitually, Counselors of level 5 or more, assist and guide for the first shifting into the gas state, but this is not a normal situation. New memory banks input: start the transition gradually with caution. One of the main rule to stay safe in gas state and alleviate many unknown factors, is staying in contact with the ground or matters attached to the ground at all time. A key safety practice.

Time has come. Evaluating: checking the air force's direction and strength, the bright star's orientation for an optimum light exposure, and distance to the objective. Proceeding. *It* starts by stretching *its* unity into a narrow shape, that way, *its* gas-vapor can hold on to the ground while the rest is finishing the process. The shifting is done relatively fast since *its* whole unity is a level 1 with no more than 314 drops of water-like, the standard size for all the *Like-It* newly created—a size carefully chosen in reference to the constant and unlimited number 3.14. The transition was well executed for a first time, alone. Satisfaction. Though, still a long path from a very experienced *Like-It* of a level 10, the maximum one with 3141 drops, who can shift *its* whole unity almost instantly. The additional drop is an acknowledgement for their great achievements and will allow their participation in the sublime creation of a newly-created, by re-sharing that extra drop. In motion. After an exponential time of cautiousness, *It* manages to reach the targets *altogether* and safely. Grand success.

There are other advantages being in the gas state. A simple touch on a potential partner captures a detailed string of data and shows a clearer compatibility view—not to mention it's the best way to accomplish a successful symbiosis. So, with a simple touch, *It* senses that these colorful matters are cold, without a consciousness and full of an empty resonance. Looked so alive but feel so dead. That's when a sound is finally heard at degree 167. Few sounds of life in fact. Checking. A life form, at last, moving with speed and agility. Relieved.

The first striking data, beside its dexterity, is the wonder of its color: orange, alike the unique star before going in hiding or when coming out of it, except for the underpart in white. Amazed. Similar to some green areas of the ground, it is totally covered with millions of a thin matter going upward and densely placed together, most likely to provide some protection to withstand the cold of the dark periods. A good sign of adaptation to its environment. This native's unity is composed of 6 parts seamlessly connected to a bigger, elongated-roundish, central one. 4 are comparable appendices, symmetrically attached to the underpart, used for the locomotion. At the end of one side, a fairly long, round, curvy part, is waving in rhythm when in motion. Possibly as a main sensor. The last part, placed at the opposite end, has an oval shape and is a lot smaller than the main one. It carries 2 small black points, equally placed on the upper part of it, pointing to the direction of its next movements. Plausibly serving as windows for its consciousness. Above each one of them, an excrescence with a deep hole, shows continuous agitation and precise reactions to sounds. An additional set of sensors. Underneath the 2 black dots, a centrally placed spot with 2 tiny holes is sporadically vibrating and seemingly reacting to the air flow. Another kind of sensor. Just beneath it, a single and small opening is processing some matter, brought from the ground with the help of the 2 front appendices. Beside the motion, the 4 appendices can apparently perform other duties. The 2 rear ones, by the long curvy part, are a little bigger than the front ones and can also serve as stabilizers, to keep its balance. A very well adapted and efficient design. The carefully chosen matters must be its main source of energy. Its inside has apparently the capabilities to convert matters into energy, confirming a synergy system on this world, even between organic and non-organic elements.

Granted, the colorful, non-mobile matters on the ground were perfect for a first try, but now there is another serious challenge: find a way to touch it. Yet, equipped with all its different sensors and speed, the projection points to a minimal percentage of success. A daunting task. On a positive note, the Orange Wonder does not seem to have detected *Its* presence while in gas state. Maybe *It* should simply re-apply what *It* just did and learned to reach it: focus, precautions, patience.
Evaluating then proceeding carefully.
Passed half way mark. Positive and controlled progression. Now, near touching distance. New data input: the force of air is suddenly becoming too erratic again. *It* has to stop and hold *its* Whole together until the air slows down. The Orange Wonder paused its intake process, all sensors reacting. The air is now delivering stronger waves. There is no more orange spot in sight. It moved so fast. The air is too strong. Safety mode required. Failed attempt.
Annoyed.

[As desolated as the view is, Life, once again, prevails, like this curious or brave or very hungry—all orange—Siberian squirrel, scouting for his meal. Gusts of wind are populating the newly free space here and there, while a spherical mist the size of a ping pong ball, is slowly rolling and ricocheting on the ground like a round bush in a ghost town, and magically turn into a small piece of ice.]

Besides providing a strong protection, the safety mode, has the particularity to keep *Like-It* between a standby and stasis state, with the consciousness reduced to a minimum and automatisms that can be preset each time, depending on the necessities of the situation. Once memory banks are set, shifting back to the liquid or gas state can happen when safety and light have been detected. *It* might look-alike a piece of random transparent ice but *It* will not melt under direct light or heat sources like frozen H2O would do.

This time, the air's instability lasted until the middle of the next light cycle. Liquid state and light-bathing have now restored *its* full alertness. Sounds of life are slowly emerging from the spared side, but from creatures that are hidden or not visible yet. The need for more encounters requires an active exploring and additional displacements. Targeting an attractive opening, between some vertical, tall, brown cylinders, to stay exposed under the light since many small green parts at their top are shading the ground. Evaluating and ready to proceed. That's when *It* saw it. It simply appeared in the opening *It* just selected, moving slowly, with confidence. The surprise is as massive as the size of this organism.

Oddly, the configuration of this impressive entity is comparable to the Orange Wonder, but it has a brown color and a mass about 200 times larger. This creature also has a main-central, cylindrical part, 4 longer appendices for self-motion, a big and strong front part with the same kind of sensors. However, something is completely different and captivating about this one. While the Orange Wonder had a very long and exuberant rear part, this Mighty One has a tiny one, but on its front part, it has an extra set of 2 protuberances, both symmetrically placed on the very top, ahead of the 2 excrescences and behind the 2 black windows. They are so wide, so overdeveloped and look so majestic that it's a puzzle as how this native is able to move and carry them around. They strikingly resemble to the higher sections of the tall brown cylinders but without the myriads of the little flat green things attached to them. Fascinated. The other surprising data is their texture, akin to the brown cylinder ones, suggesting a deeper synergy or even some form of symbiosis. Unexpected.

Optimism is now flirting with all *its* cells after this incredible appearance, comforted that this world is in fact, fertile and filled with diverse life forms. The decision to sense this mighty entity is an obvious one since *It* was about to move in that direction anyway. Re-evaluating and ready to proceed again.

After a flawless shift in the gas state, *It* is now surfing the ground toward the new found prize, with an increased confidence, focusing on the next potential grip, and tasting this exhilarating exposure. Meanwhile, Mighty One is processing with constancy, in its dedicated opening, the green matter picked up directly from the ground.

Arriving at the opening, safely and undetected. Contentment. Now, selecting the best approach to touch it. Logically, from the rear, at the opposite end of all its sensors, to augment the percentage of success. Softly gliding and finally, contact.

Warmth and strength. Climbing on one of the 2 rear appendices and pausing at the top. Everything is crude strength, like its 2 protuberances projected on the outside. Impressive. The main-central part is essentially a medium soft container, holding many pieces of different shapes and sizes, working seemingly together. Hardened pieces present in all of the 6 major parts help support most of the soft substance. The entire being is enclosed in an envelope that also act as a protective shell from the external conditions, as noted with Orange Wonder. Inside, something is pulsating repeatedly, sending a vibrant echo all over its structure. Some fluids, running in tiny conducts spreaded everywhere, are fluctuating in rhythm with that pulse. This alien is even more alive inside than outside. Unsuspected. The complexity of its internal world is a lot more disturbing than its environment. Baffled. Wondering what would happen to the whole unity if just one of the parts inside is missing or malfunctioning since they are in a complex and balanced assembly. Interestingly, Orange Wonder was processing matter using a similar method, so it must be the standard practice for the local organisms. Evolution certainly found this solution to provide for their energy need—explaining how its warmth is produced and maintained.

As previously thought, the front sensors provide data of the outside conditions but to a distinctive hub, also located in the front part, behind the 2 black windows. This unique hub is made of a different matter, with millions of compact clusters exchanging intense and fast electrical signals. Some of these signals are in turn, forwarded throughout its unity, via a specific network. Probably transmitting instructions to the other parts. All of this implies that its consciousness reside solely in this hub, acting as the control center. Maybe a direct contact with the hub or network could help decipher the meaning of these electrical impulses. For that, the use of one of the front sensors' hole as an entrance, to find a connecting point and secure a safer shelter, is evident. This native might not be the perfect choice, without knowing the level of its consciousness, but it feels safe enough for a temporary symbiosis. Its strength, warmth, mobility and immense energy will also help greatly for discovering further on.
Sliding toward the front, smoothly and optimistically undetected. Mighty One is unexpectedly halting his green matter's harvest off the ground, and raised its bulged front part very high, holding still. Pausing too, possibly been detected. When side sounds are heard, Mighty One hurdled ahead so forcefully that the air around *It* turned into a spinning current, sending *It* up high before gravity slowly wins again. Mighty One is surely gone now. Another Setback. Disappointed.

Landing on the ground, a little further in the opening, near a large spherical assemblage of mixed green and brown matters that is trembling irregularly. Hesitant. Investigate or safety state? Sometimes, curiosity can be an ally and this time, connecting rapidly is paramount if a new encounter shows potential. Moving around the spherical assemblage to see the cause of the shaking.

There, a new creature, different than the first 2, shaped in curves, is standing pretty high. A sight of magnificence. Mostly in pure white color this time, except for the bottom segments of its 2 appendices, and half of the front part—in dark pink. The opening that processed matter on the first 2, is now very elongated and all black. The particular arrangement of the colors are emphasizing the strange shape of this one, configured undoubtedly for a specific purpose. The section between the central oval part and the small front part seems to be stretched, as if the smaller front part wanted to go faster than the rest. This creature must excel at going forward very fast, but also defies logic with only 2 very thin appendices to keep its equilibrium. Its white envelope has no visible openings and appears to be sealed from external interferences, optimized to evade anything resistive to its progression—a general feel of speed and fragility, in a specialized design.

Its elongated opening is now searching the ground, covered with thin water, for the right matter to process. It's the small rear part, touching the large spherical assemblage that is causing the occasional sounds and shakings.

Approaching to make contact, using the spherical assemblage to access its rear side. Climbing. Undetected yet. Contact made with the white envelope. Nothing. Expected and confirms the previous observations. The dark pink areas should reveal something. Moving hastily toward the front part, raised again, for sensing. Reaching the dark pink from underneath. Contact is effective this time. Lower strength and warmth, but same principles as Mighty One for the internal parts and for the matter processed into energy. The echo of the steady pulse is a lot softer, without vibrations. It does have 4 appendices but it's only using 2 for self-motion, the other 2 are folded within the white cover. They are different than the 2 visible ones, for a purpose unknown. The special hub, full of electrical signals too, is right here, behind the 2 small windows and sensors. That short distance from one of the sensors' openings will facilitate its access and connection with. Stretching *its* gas unity, to stay aware of the outside world and for orientation while inside.

[In a matter of seconds, a reindeer enters a glade calmly, a tiny spherical mist is gliding on his back, the reindeer precipitately disappears in the forest, and the tiny mist lends nearby a busy white crane.]

Entering. Testing the bacterial photosynthesis immediately. Very high compatibility, excellent level of efficiency. Immensely relieved. Successful symbiosis in progress. The first one, done all alone. The equation should remain positive from this point.

A prompt comparison between the 2 photosynthesis is inevitable. The pleasant energy flow coming from the bacteria might demand more involvement than the one received directly from the light sources, but its steadiness and the shelter found within the partner make it a secure choice. Amplified confidence.
Searching for a nearby connection point to either the hub or the network, to evaluate the level of consciousness. In the meantime, Magnificent White continues to collect and process matters without any signs of disturbance. A converging point of the hub and network is found, with electrical signals going in both directions. Securing the grip of *its* cells on the inside walls and stand ready for the alien's electrical signal input. Connecting to the network first. Signals accepted. Weaker but faster than anticipated. Adjusting and analyzing. No recognizable data. Signals are identical and rapid. Must be routine directives. Observing. Time is passing with no changes. Magnificent White is still collecting matters. The hub might give readable and instructive data. Disconnecting and preparing for the hub link. Connecting. Denser and busier. The hub is totally different than the other internal parts, it is a whole world in itself. Signals are running everywhere, diligent and restless. Decrypting them. No data understandable either, not enough to gauge its consciousness accurately.
After analyzing for some time, no detectable signs of social communications, ongoing mathematics researches or traces of an advanced civilization. This native is simply focused on basic survival. Its behavior is guided by its instinct, not by a higher

conscience. Even so, Magnificent White is a suitable partner, found at the right time, until a new innate with higher potential is met. Displacements and safety are now depending on its choices and self-preservation abilities, but for the moment, storing energy remains its priority.

The dark cycle is coming slowly, and this time, *its* consciousness will remain fully alert until the next light cycle. Contented. Magnificent White is in motion now, the outside temperature is dropping gradually and the dark is imposing its restricted conditions. Soon, Magnificent White stops under a dense area of green matters and starts circling right where it is standing, again and again, folds its 2 visible appendices, bringing the central part and the front part together on the ground, immobile, hidden behind the density. Its whole unity is slowly reducing its inside activities to a slower pace. Then, its hub entered a different state. Surprised.
It is wondering if it's a form of standby mode, if the dark has this effect on all the creatures of this world or just this particular one. The darkness is apparently a universal handicap. Magnificent White will most certainly stay in this mode every time, until the bright star is back. Consequently, this symbiosis will be limited by some of this alien's constraints, but *It* can use the pausing time to launch mathematical assessments, updates or create new equations about this experience and organize them in *its* memory banks in case another *Like-It* reappears.

Few time units before the full light, when the higher view is still all orange, Magnificent White's hub emerges from the standby mode, followed by the whole unity. Switching to the displacement mode, it rises the central part up with the 2 main appendices, finds its balance inexplicably again, and moves toward a not so high green area covered with a thin layer of water. There, it slowly processes some matters, replenishes its water level and shows another surprise. The unfolding of the other 2 appendices. They are completely different, very long, with a surface few times larger than its whole unity and shaped awkwardly, maybe for speed too. The newly exposed area underneath is all black and must be a different kind of protective layer. It starts to rub and sprinkle water on the black layer first, with its elongated opening, then, to any area it could reach. When done, it shakes its whole unity, fold them back in place and simply continues the collect-process occupation. Its energy need must require a regular amount of collected matter. During all that time, comfortably set in this new symbiosis, *It* is adapting to these new rhythms of life, observing and learning more about this estranged world.

When the bright star reaches the highest point, Magnificent White suddenly stops its main occupation. It rises its front part up high, waits as if it's sensing the surroundings, assessing the current conditions, emits a series of strange sounds coming from the lower part of the elongated opening, and unfold the 2 extra appendices again. Startled. These sounds sent uncomfortable vibrations all over the front part, disturbing *its* clarity. Re-stabilized in a fraction of time, *It* is now witnessing and experiencing directly, another unsuspected wonder. The 2 extra appendices, now open wide, are in an up and down oscillation while Magnificent White starts to move forward faster and faster, making a "splash" sound each time one of the 2 main appendices touches the water-ground, until the sound of the splashes fades and is replaced by a "flap-flap" sound now coming from the 2 extra ones. At that moment, Magnificent White is separated from the ground. Able to keep a stable course while surfing and playing with the force of air to go higher, glide or change direction, by simply using the 2 extra appendices, for propulsion and control. Overwhelmed. Magnificent White deserves its name, not only for its shapes or colors, but also for the ingenuity of its design and the efficiency of all its parts. Its ability to choose between 2 types of motions, with 2 different pairs of appendices, each conceived for either the ground or the air motion, is the proof of a long and tested evolution, resulting in this 2 in 1 being. A marvel. It's obvious now that its shapes and contours are primary made for the air motion, where it can express its full potential. The 2 appendices for the ground are in fact secondary, and serve only to help collecting matters and water while the true prominent ones are folded, for an increased protection when not in use. Not evolved for the flatness of the 2 dimensions but for the volume of the 3 dimensions.

From high above, the view is very global, challenging and strange. Sorrow. The Vessel might have experienced it upon its arrival on the planet. Everything underneath is a mix of green and brown matters with water. It's not easy to decide if water was here first or if the brown and green matters were. Being at peace with the force of air, using it as an ally for displacements, is a new and comforting sensation. Gratitude. After surfing the air with dexterity for some time, the orange color from the escaping bright star announces the coming of the dark period. Magnificent White is reducing its distance with the ground. The darker it gets, the closer it surfs. It chooses a welcome zone under many medium-high combinations of green and brown matters, with nearby water. Having collected some matters, replenished its water level, found a place to rest, it starts the circling protocol, folds its whole unity tightly and switches to the standby mode. Again, it's the perfect moment to try to understand the mystery of the sudden departure, and its destination.

When the light cycle is slowly restoring its temporary presence, with the orange color as its ambassador, Magnificent White activates its hub, harvests matters and water, emits the destabilizing sounds, unfolds, splashes, flap-flaps and surfs the air again. These precise practices are certainly a necessity before every new light cycle's journey, but the reason for the strange sounds remains inexplicable yet.
Several repetitive light and dark cycles passed, when in the middle of a new light period, the air ahead is blocked by an enormous, suspended, grey matter. The distance between the ground and the suspended grey matter is many times below Magnificent White, and that grey matter is spreading a lot higher than its current trajectory. As it comes closer, it starts to surf downward but enters the grey density anyway. Surprisingly, no changes are perceived from the

reaction of its internal parts and surf's stability. Beside the no view at all, *It* only notices a major increase in the density of the tiny drops of water suspended in the air, alike *its* gas state. Interesting phenomenon. Once through, the view underneath the grey density is back to normal but not as bright. Few big drops of water start to fall off the density, then millions, probably too heavy to stay suspended. Magnificent White continues its surfing well after the drops stop falling and until the light cycle ends.

In the early time of the following light period, between few disparate, white groups of suspended drops of water, something amazing and highly coveted appeared in sight. Signs of a developed civilization. Symmetrical portions of the ground are filled with symmetrical structures of different sizes, shapes, heights and colors. Although too high in the air to see the appearance of the new beings, these signs of diversity already show a great consciousness. Long straight links on the ground, with tiny objects or inhabitants on them, are connecting the structures from distant areas. Observing from this high view should reveal precious data before a close encounter. Enthusiastic. During the rest of the cycle, big or small clusters of structures are separated by large zones of mixed green and brown matters or sometimes, by simply green ones. Since the high view is clear again, the orange color is back everywhere before the dark replaces it. *It* is now anticipating if Magnificent White will touch the ground nearby or away from the structures. The result is at 90 percent away, reducing the possibilities to see these beings before the next light. Very soon, Magnificent White's choice confirms the projection, away and too far from any structures.

During the next light, the clusters of structures are closer to each other and becoming bigger and denser. Though the surfing is still too high for more details, the number of these beings and the surface occupied is imposing. This species is most certainly the dominant one on this huge planet. At around 3/4 into the light cycle, formations of white suspended drops of water are seen everywhere above the ongoing trajectory, darkening a little the remaining

surfing time. Progressively, artificial lights are turned on inside the structures and on each sides of the main links before the dark cycle is well in place. It's after some time that *It* realizes the light cycle seems to last longer and Magnificent White is extending its surfing. Even if the bright star should not be visible by now, the consistent light coming from the white suspended formations is bright enough to think that the light cycle is still here. The logical explanation is the start of a new rhythm between the light and dark.
Magnificent White is showing symptoms of discomfort. Its internal pulse is faster and its surfing is not always balanced. The added surfing time is surely depleting its energy and water reserves. Touching the ground is becoming a priority but structures are everywhere on the surface. A narrow and curvy path of water is passing through the center of a very large cluster. Many previously passed clusters had a path of water too, suggesting that these beings have similar intake needs as Magnificent White does. It skillfully negotiate a sharp angle toward the path of water, targeting the side with the brown and greenest matters on it, away from the nearest structure. Reducing the speed, in stopping posture, then reunited with the ground, by the water. Its internal rhythm is fast and it starts gathering water immediately, before any matters. After the water duty, it raises its front part high for sensing, giving *It* a wider view to assess the surroundings. A new inhabitant, most likely one of the beings, is coming this direction. Pleased and intrigued. It is high, higher than Magnificent White, with 6 different parts. It also uses 2 long appendices for the ground displacement, has the central part rectangular with 2 extra, medium long, appendices attached on each side by the top, and a big round part, centrally placed at the very top. That round part has the same kind of sensors Orange Wonder has, all placed similarly but with different shapes. Behind the 2 windows, a hub is certainly harboring the great consciousness. Its envelope must be fragile because almost all of its unity is behind a layer of foreign matters, including the top of the round part. Only the tiny space between the lower opening and the air sensor, is covered with thousands of the thin matter going outward. The Being halts its progression by a low, symmetrical construction, on which it folds

itself halfway and direct its 2 windows upward. This is the opportunity *It* has been searching for, but abandoning Magnificent White is not easy. It has provided steady energy, protection, motion in an unexpected form and discovery of this world. On the minus side, it has a basic consciousness, requires a standby mode time, emits disturbing sounds and is pursuing an unknown objective. This new being shows physical abilities and has a higher consciousness, both too appealing to not take the risk. Moving forward.

Once the decision is taken, and before the front part goes down again to harvest matters, *It* is floating in the air. Like *It* was never there. And since the force of air is somewhere else, *Its* weightlessness unity slowly reaches the ground and begins the slide toward *its* future partner.

Wonderings

Sitting at the sunny terrace of a recently opened tea shop, watching the vibrant flow of life while sipping a freshly arrived Indian tea, he's wondering if there will be enough clouds tonight to witness the singularity again. Then he thinks: "Maybe I should read the entire newspaper properly this time, I must have missed an article mentioning it somewhere within all these pages." And grumbling: "This is not a common event, you would think they would have printed it on the front page as the headlines!" When he turns to page four, he finds it, printed as an ordinary article: "...night skies over Europe and western Russia glowed brightly enough for people to read by." It's a half-page long paragraph, explaining the whole event. He wonders again how he could have missed it. Nonetheless, the whole thing started two nights ago, like the fireman said, confirming that the cause is not the aurora borealis he first thought of but high altitude clouds carrying dust and possibly thin ice particles, thus increasing the reflection effect. These elements were traveling west from Siberia where a massive and unexplained explosion happened some ten days ago. Three Russian newspapers are cited, describing part of the event. The *Sibir newspaper* wrote: "...peasants observed high above the horizon, some strangely bright (impossible to look at) bluish-white heavenly body, which for 10 minutes moved downwards. The body appeared as a "pipe", i.e., a cylinder... As the body neared the ground (forest), the bright body seemed to smudge, and then turned into a giant billow of black smoke, and a loud knocking (not thunder) was heard, as if large stones were falling, or artillery was fired. All buildings shook. At the same time the cloud began emitting flames of uncertain shapes." "Pretty impressive" he thought. From the second newspaper, the *Krasnoyaretz newspaper*: "An unusual atmospheric event was observed. ...noise akin to a strong wind was heard. Immediately afterwards a horrific thump sounded, followed by an earthquake that literally shook the buildings. ...the interval between the first and the third thumps were accompanied by an unusual underground rattle, similar to a railway upon which dozens of trains are travelling at the same time. Afterwards for 5 to 6 minutes an exact likeness of artillery fire was heard: 50 to 60 salvoes in short, equal intervals, which got progressively weaker. ...more thumps were heard, like cannon firing, but individual, loud and accompanied by tremors. ...upon closer inspection to the north, i.e. where most of the thumps were heard, a kind of an ashen cloud was seen near the horizon." The last one, The *Siberian Life newspaper* mentioned: "When the meteorite fell, strong tremors in the ground were observed ...two strong explosions were heard, as if from large-caliber artillery." "Definitively fascinating!" he said out loud. Now thinking: "They think it's a meteorite, that sounds like a plausible explanation but it must have been a rather big one." Trying to envision the catastrophic consequences if it had fallen on Moscow or St. Petersburg. Then, as usual, he simply decides to let his scientific mind feed on these incredible details. The causes for such loud and scary sounds are mostly due to the sudden conflict in temperatures when it entered the atmosphere at high speed, braking into many smaller parts, which in turn, broke into smaller pieces and so on. The description of a "body appeared as a pipe, a cylinder" is surely the most intriguing part of the entire testimony since a cylinder looks more of a manufactured object than just a random meteorite. If this is the case, what could it be? Who can fly an object that high? Who could have designed it? How was it built? What went wrong? The scope of this hypothesis is almost frightening. Or, maybe it was simply a meteorite, falling as it happened all the time, but this one was big enough to be noticed.

With these enigmatic propositions in mind, he spends most of the day attending his errands, then comes back home to change for the evening's concert. Once dressed, and having enough time ahead of the Mozart's violin sonata, one of his favorite, he decides to take a walk by the river's banks to observe the clouds' glowing effect.

Approaching the Being rapidly. Reaching the low structure. The Being's round part is still directed upward. Climbing the structure first, then from the back of the Being. No reactions, still undetected and no direct contact with the envelope yet. Magnificent White decides to make louder sounds with its air appendices. The Being turns its round part toward it and stay immobile. Probably assessing the situation. After few time units, the Being returns its round part to the upward direction. Relieved. Progressing again. At the top of the rectangle part, next to the round part, *It* can now touch the envelope directly. Contact. No surprise, warmth, fluids and electrical signals. The different internal parts are operating in a similar way as the first 2, but with a medium echo from the regular pulse and a hub many times more active. Excitement.

Entering by the side sensor to establish a connection with the hub. Stretching *its* unity to reach it behind a hard wall. Connecting directly to it this time. Super nova effect. Retreating and reorganizing. Not cautious enough. The hub's signals are very strong. Consolidating *its* stance and pre-adjusting to the strength, intensity and speed of this foreign electrical signal before attempting another contact. Ready to proceed. Connecting. Exponentially more complex than Magnificent White. An inside galaxy, full of minuscule bright stars, all linked and constantly communicating with each other with billions of electrical signals. An organized chaos. A splendor in a confined space but with a sense of unlimited potential. A vision, a choreography worth of all the tryouts, perilous space travels, consumed energy, curiosity, projections, attempts, failures, losses. Astonished. Still, unreadable data, except for some stronger signals, interpreted as brutal glimpses of basic emotions. Somewhat positive and perhaps the first step to a communication link. Analyzing, modulating and testing this alien signals. Not enough key data perceived to begin translating them. Observing and learning. Few time units passes when the Being moves its round part down and starts to fold one of its top appendices between the layers

of the protective matter, but instead, takes it out right away with something attached at the end of it. That's when *It* realizes that the extremities of the 2 top appendices have the ability to hold and manipulate things with dexterity. Another great freedom. Then, using these both extremities, it holds a small and thin rectangular white matter on one side, while the other side holds a thin, round and long black matter to apply some marks on the white one. The marks show a circle with 2 straight lines intersecting on its center at a 90 degree angle. The being continues marking down smaller marks of different strains, in successive lines, as a mathematic equation would be. It is researching for a mathematic solution of an enigma it just marked down. Immense joy. A well-developed civilization is aware that the Mathematics are universal and central to its advancement. This species obviously used calculation and projections to build the surrounding structures. Impressed.
Yet, *It* is wondering why the Being needs to mark a mathematic equation on an external support to complete the research? With its ultra-active hub, the results should be faster if done from the inside. Unless its hub does not have the memory capacity embedded in the cells. If so, how does this species store data and transfer knowledge to the newly-created? Is the use of external supports always necessary? More data will be needed for an accurate conclusion.

After many unsuccessful attempts to translate the meaning of these marks and to interpret the electrical signals, *It* recognizes that the Great Abandon might be the only path to possibly understand these beings. Magnificent White was also unreadable but did not show the same potential this Being does. Reaching this level of evolution is a fantastic burst of life in the harsh conditions and coldness of the Big Empty. Encountering the first alien species with the self-conscience ability and the understanding of the Mathematics demands persistence. The desire and curiosity to learn more about this fascinating species, the fact that *It* is certainly the last one active on this world, are all the right reasons leading to this risky decision. It is called the Great Abandon because of the uncertainty of the outcome. When a *Like-It* is totally immersed inside a partner, without stretching *its* unity to stay in contact with the exterior, *It* can lose *its* Whole, *its* alertness, after many time units. Both alien cells could fusion together and initiate the ultimate symbiosis. And, if the partner's life ends, either of age or by accident, *It* would dilute with it.

Still, the knowledge offset the risk.
Bringing *its* whole unity inside.
Spreading and wrapping around the hub.
Adjusting and adapting.
In full symbiosis.

Epiphany

He arrives at the Aare River with plenty of time left, so he starts following the curves of the west bank, walking on the grass and smelling the vegetation's humidity as a welcome treat. It's supposed to be dark already but the glowing clouds are dispensing their strange light everywhere, giving the atmosphere the feel of an overcast day. By the end of the curve, he sees an empty bench, near the water, and a beautiful white crane lending not far from it. "These birds have such a majestic stance and grace." The crane is already drinking water. "It must have been a long journey for this long distance flyer." When he stops by the bench, he simply sits and looks up to admire the glowing show. Few minutes later, the crane is making some noise with its wings, apparently enjoying this much awaited bath. Back to the clouds' mystery, his scientific mind cannot stop being impressed by the magnitude of "the cylinder's explosion" and the extent of its consequences. So many particles are travelling within all these clouds that the size of the cylinder must have been quite substantial. He's wondering if he can calculate its size by evaluating the mass of these particles. He reaches his left internal pocket to grab the small notebook he always carries with him and start drawing a circle and write some equations. Several minutes passes when a bell's chime reminds him that the concert will start soon.

On his way to the concert hall, he's thinking about the noctilucent clouds, the cylinder's size and explosion, the energy, the mass, the particles, the properties of the light, the effects of the temperatures and gravity, all kind of equations, when an unusual clarity of mind allows him to experience an exciting intuition, like an epiphany. That idea would bring all theories from different fields, under a unified one that could explain all.

Upon his arrival at the concert hall, a smiling host greats him:
"Good evening sir, and welcome to our concert of the evening."
"Tonight, we will be playing a violin sonata of the great Mozart!"
"May I ask for your invitation sir?"
Then, with a smile, he replies:
"Good evening to you sir."
"Well, I do not have an invitation with me but my name should be noted on the list."
"I'm Albert Einstein."

Notes:

Although best known for his E=Mc2, his "theory of relativity," his 1921 Nobel Prize in Physics and the Manhattan Project, Professor Albert Einstein (1879-1955) worked very hard during his life, on his idea of ONE "unified fields theory" that would explain all.

Until now, his brain remains a mystery as why it was still in the healthy state of a 25 years old man when he died at age 76...

It is interesting to note that Albert Einstein was born on a March, 14th (1879), or what we celebrate nowadays as the "Pi day" for the number 3.14, which has a special meaning for the Photans.

Throughout human history, many great minds mentioned an "abstract guidance" leading them to great discoveries.
Maybe a Photan was "accompanying" them, maybe not...

As you noticed, I tried to "visually" emphasize the alien aspect by using the right alignment, and accentuate their worship to mathematics by using real numbers instead of letters. Humans remained on the left alignment when any attempt of symbiosis was centered.

Photan: pho·tan
noun \ˈfō-ˌtän
A liquid based, state-shifter alien species. Origin unknown.

Disclaimer:

For those who still don't believe Humans actually did land on the moon, this is not a conspiracy theory nor an attempt to diminish Doctor Albert Einstein's abilities, work and achievements.

This fictional novelette is for entertainment purpose only, so please, don't stop enjoying the steam rooms!

Work in progress:

I imagined this novelette like an episode of "The Twilight Zone" or "The Outer limits" TV series, but was intended to introduce one element (the Photans) of my upcoming series called "Healers."

(Novels)
HEALERS
(Part I, II, III…)

(Short story)
Immobile immortality

www.AlexPusineri.com

www.ingramcontent.com/pod-product-compliance
Lightning Source LLC
Chambersburg PA
CBHW030419160726
47992CB00007B/3193